THE STORYBOOK
BASED ON THE
MOVIE

Random House 🏠 New York

Based on the film *Willow*

Story by George Lucas
Screenplay by Bob Dolman

Storybook adaptation by
Cathy East Dubowski

Library of Congress Cataloging-in-Publication Data:
Willow : the storybook based on the movie. p. cm. SUMMARY: A poor farmer undertakes a mission to find safety for a baby destined to be a great queen but now in danger from an evil sorceress. ISBN: 0-394-89574-6 (pbk.); 0-394-99574-0 (lib. bdg.) [1. Fantasy.] PZ7.W68385 1988 [Fic.]—dc19 88-1942

Manufactured in the United States of America 1 2 3 4 5 6 7 8 9 0

Willow: A Nelwyn farmer and would-be magician

Sorsha: Queen Bavmorda's daughter

Madmartigan: A renegade warrior and expert swordsman

Rool and Franjean: Two mischievous brownies

Elora Danan: An infant girl, born to fulfill an ancient prophecy

Cherlindrea: The fairy queen

The High Aldwin: A Nelwyn sorcerer

Queen Bavmorda: The evil sorceress who rules Nockmaar

Fin Raziel: A good sorceress

Many years ago, in a strange and magical land, there lived a heartless queen named Bavmorda. She ruled cruelly from dark Nockmaar Castle, high in the volcanic mountains. All feared her, for she was a powerful sorceress, but none had the might to defeat her army of soldiers and dreaded killer beasts known as Death Dogs. Only a small rebel army challenged her rule.

On the day this story begins, however, there was a feeling in the air . . . a feeling of change and a feeling of coming danger. A guard in the tower fidgeted as he stood in endless watch. A mountain lion paced restlessly, as if sensing something was about to happen—something that would change forever the lives of all creatures in this troubled world.

Suddenly a woman's cries rang out from the depths of the castle's dungeon. And then, after a time, a new sound pierced the air: the first cry of a newborn baby.

It was a beautiful baby girl, and her mother, filled with joy, hugged her tight. But the baby was not an ordinary child, for on her arm was a strange birthmark. When the mother saw it, she wept with both joy and sorrow. An ancient prophecy had foretold that the child born with this mark would bring about the defeat of evil Queen Bavmorda and grow up to be a good, wise queen herself.

But how can she? wondered the mother. *She is the queen's prisoner. . . .*

Within minutes of the birth, Princess Sorsha, the queen's auburn-haired daughter, pushed past the guards into the dungeon's dirty, cramped jail cell. "Is it a girl?" she asked.

"Yes, Your Highness," said the midwife who had delivered the child.

"Show me its arm!" Sorsha demanded. She peered down at the tiny, pink baby, lying among the rags next to her mother. "She bears the birthmark—the prophecy has begun! I must tell the queen immediately." And Sorsha hurried up the dungeon stairs toward the light.

The midwife washed the baby, then began to wrap it in clean rags. The mother, weak from childbirth, clutched at the midwife's skirts.

"Ethna—please help me! They're going to kill my baby!"

"Hush!" Ethna whispered harshly, eying the guards nearby. Then she added more gently, "I'm sorry . . . but Queen Bavmorda will kill anyone who goes against her."

Exhausted, the mother sank back into her bed of rags. But still she begged, "Save my baby! Take her away. Please!"

Ethna hesitated. She was a poor, humble midwife. She shouldn't get involved, she told herself. She shouldn't risk her own life! Then she looked at the mother's frantic, pleading eyes. She looked into the fresh, pink face of the innocent child. And she looked at the weapons in the hands of the cruel guards.

She knew she had to help.

Quickly she tied some rags into the shape of a baby and placed the bundle in the mother's arms. Then she hid the baby in a basket of rags and hurried up the stairs past the guards, tightly clutching the basket in her trembling hands.

Moments later boot steps rang out upon the stone steps. Queen Bavmorda swept down the dungeon stairs, her black robes sailing out behind her. Sorsha followed, barely able to keep up with her mother.

"So!" said Bavmorda smugly. "*Your* baby is the great queen who supposedly will destroy me?"

"Yes!" cried the child's mother. "But nothing you can do will change the prophecy!"

"We shall see about that. . . . Start the ritual!" Bavmorda shouted with a wave of her hand. "I shall destroy this child—she will have no power over me!" The queen snatched the bundle from the mother's arms and began to tear it apart. Then she realized—she was holding nothing but rags!

"Where is it?" Queen Bavmorda sputtered furiously, roughly shoving the mother aside to search her bed.

"The midwife!" cried Sorsha. "She must have taken the baby!"

Bavmorda's eyes flashed, and she shook with rage. "Find that baby, Sorsha! Take the Death Dogs! A thousand soldiers! Just bring her back to me alive!"

Sorsha obediently charged up the stairs.

"Your reign of terror is at an end!" cried the baby's mother. "My daughter will destroy you! You can't stop her!"

Bavmorda turned toward the stairs. "Kill her," she ordered the guards, and left the dungeon without a backward glance.

War drums were beating. The shouts of guards and the hungry growls of Death Dogs filled the air. Not far from the castle Ethna heard the chase begin, and she fled, terrified, into an unknown wilderness.

For days she ran, seldom eating, barely closing her eyes even in the dark of night, as the distant barking filled her waking dreams. She struggled through snow, hid in villages, trekked across open grassland, all the while caring for the tiny child as best she could. The days turned into weeks, the weeks into months. And still Queen Bavmorda's soldiers pursued them.

Then one day Ethna heard the dogs closer than ever. She scrambled across a shallow river. Frantically she tore

away sticks and driftwood to fashion a crude little raft, then gently laid the baby inside. She had grown to love this hunted child, but she was running out of strength. And now there was no time to think, nowhere to hide. Sobbing, she pushed the tiny raft into the river's swirling current.

With a sudden howl two Death Dogs raced out of the woods and splashed across the stream. As they lunged for Ethna, the baby floated safely out of sight.

Alone now, the baby drifted far downstream. The water rocked her mud-and-stick raft so gently that she might have been in a cradle, and she slept peacefully for a long time. Then a sharp turn in the river sent the raft swirling toward the bank, where it caught among the reeds.

The baby woke with a tiny coo.

On the riverbank something rustled in the bushes. But it was not a Death Dog or a soldier. Peeking through the reeds were two very small children. For the raft had come to rest in Nelwyn country, a land of hardworking little people who believed in the ways of magic. The Nelwyns lived peacefully in their tiny corner of the world, keeping to themselves, doing nothing to attract the anger of Queen Bavmorda and her soldiers, who towered like giants over them.

The children whispered excitedly

to each other as they stared at the strange baby. Then they ran off, calling for their father.

Nearby, Willow Ufgood struggled to hold on to a plow that a huge pig was dragging across his half-plowed land. Willow awkwardly tossed seed over his shoulder into a ragged furrow. But he smiled when his children ran up.

"Hurry, Dada!" shouted his son, Ranon.

"Come to the river!" cried his daughter, Mims.

"I can't play with you now. I'm too busy," said Willow.

"But we found something you must see!" Ranon insisted.

With a sigh Willow dropped his seed sack. Mims ran ahead as Ranon tugged their father along by the sleeve.

At the river Ranon pulled the reeds aside, and Mims dragged the little raft onto the bank.

At the sight of the baby Willow began to shout, "Mims! Get back! It might bite! We don't know where it's been! It could be diseased!"

"What is it, Dada?" asked Mims. "It's not a Nelwyn."

Willow shook his head. "No, it's much too big. It looks like—a Daikini baby! I wonder what it's doing here. . . ."

The children squealed with delight. They had often heard spine-tingling tales of the strange, giant Daikinis, who lived far beyond their village, but they had never actually seen one.

"It's such a pretty baby," said Mims.

"Can we keep it?" begged Ranon.

"Absolutely not!" said Willow. "Nelwyns have no business meddling in the affairs of giants. Now, push it downstream—and forget we ever saw it!"

Just then shouts rang out from the nearby field. "Willow! Willow Ufgood, you scoundrel! Where are you?"

Willow groaned. That quarrelsome voice could only belong to one person: Burglekutt, the bad-tempered head of the village council. And it could only mean trouble. "Stay here," Willow told his children, "and keep that thing quiet!"

Burglekutt spotted Willow dashing for his plow, and he hobbled toward him, angrily waving his stick in the air. Chasing after him was Willow's wife, Kiaya.

"Mr. Burglekutt, Willow has stolen nothing!" she insisted.

Burglekutt scooped a handful of seeds out of Willow's sack and furiously shook them under Willow's nose. "Ufgood! You haven't paid your debts to me! Where'd you get these seeds!"

"Maybe I used my magic," said

Willow defiantly. He could often be found practicing magic, for he dreamed of becoming an apprentice to the village magician.

Burglekutt laughed. "You're no magician—you're a clown! *I* sell the seeds around here. Now, where did you get these?"

Proudly Willow put his arm around his wife. "My family has been gathering seeds in the forest since last fall," he said. "There's no law against that."

In the distance the children laughed. "Willow!" cried Kiaya. "Did you leave the children alone by the river?" Alarmed, she ran toward the sound.

But Burglekutt wasn't through with Willow. "You'll *need* magic if you expect to get your planting done before the rains start!" he said. Then he grabbed Willow by the collar. "You'll lose your land to me, Ufgood, and you'll end up working in the mines!" Arrogantly he turned with his nose in the air—and tripped right over the pig.

* * *

At the river Willow found Kiaya cradling the Daikini baby in her arms. "We can't keep this baby—it's too dangerous," he said. "What if its parents come looking for it? I absolutely forbid this family to become involved!"

"Oh, Willow . . ." Kiaya said as she walked past him toward home, with Mims and Ranon fairly dancing behind her.

"Kiaya!" cried Willow, chasing after them. "Put that baby down! Mims! Ranon! I will not be ignored! . . ."

At home Kiaya bathed the baby while Willow paced the floor. Tomorrow was the annual festival to celebrate spring planting. The High Aldwin, the Nelwyns' sorcerer, was expected to pick an apprentice. And more than anything, Willow wanted to be the one he picked.

"This is bad, Kiaya," he said. "If we're caught with this baby, it'll be the end of us. Nelwyns don't like Daikinis—they don't trust them. People will think this baby's sudden

appearance is a bad omen! Then if there's a flood or a drought, they'll blame me!"

"Willow, calm down. . . ."

"But tomorrow's my big day!"

"The High Aldwin hasn't picked a new apprentice in years," Kiaya reminded him.

"Tomorrow will be different. I'm *sure* he's going to pick me! And this baby is not going to ruin it!"

Willow's shouting made the baby cry. "Calm yourself," said Kiaya.

"And hold her while I get some milk."

"I don't want to hold her," said Willow. "I don't want anything to do with her!"

But as soon as he took her, she stopped crying.

"She likes you, Dada!" said Ranon.

The baby laughed. And despite himself, Willow smiled.

The next day the Nelwyn landscape erupted in celebration. For in this village of hardworking miners and

farmers, a holiday was not to be wasted! Everyone danced and ate good food and played tug of war. On a small stage Willow tried to please a rowdy crowd with his magic act.

His show was going well, but he couldn't resist doing one last trick. For this trick he wore the magic cloak that Kiaya had made for him. It had a special secret pocket sewn into the lining.

"And now," he shouted, "I will make an entire pig disappear!" The crowd hooted and hollered as Mims and Ranon tugged a grumpy-looking piglet onto the stage.

Willow waved his cloak. "Whuppity bairn, deru, deru!" he intoned.

And the piglet was gone!

The crowd was impressed—until the squealing piglet wriggled from the secret pocket of the cloak and leaped offstage.

Willow felt foolish, and his face burned with embarrassment. The crowd laughed and booed, and then wandered off.

Suddenly trumpets blared across the village square.

"Attention!" announced a councilman. "The High Aldwin is about to choose a new apprentice. Bring forth the hopefuls!"

A crowd gathered. Willow and two others stepped forward.

Burglekutt roared with laughter. "Willow Ufgood? A hopeful? Is this a joke?"

Then the High Aldwin spoke: "Magic is the bloodstream of the universe. It is mysterious, and yet there is no mystery—mysteriously enough. Forget all you know or think you know. All that you require is your intuition." He held up his hand. "The power to control the world is in which finger?"

The first hopeful pointed nervously to the High Aldwin's index finger. The magician shook his head. The second hopeful chose the High Aldwin's middle finger. Wrong again.

Now it was Willow's turn. He hesitated, as if trying to make up his mind. So much depended on his choice! Then he took a deep breath and picked the High Aldwin's ring finger.

The sorcerer shook his head sadly and pounded his staff upon the wooden platform. "No apprentice this year!" he cried.

Burglekutt chortled. The crowd chattered excitedly.

Suddenly someone screamed. Parents grabbed their children.

A huge Death Dog ran through the crowd!

It ransacked huts and turned over wagons, biting anyone who tried to stop it. Finally Vohnkar the warrior killed it.

In the silent moment that followed, a terrified woman picked up the pieces of a broken cradle. "Look!" she cried. "It was searching for somebody's baby!"

Kiaya! thought Willow. Alarmed, he and his children ran home, afraid to imagine what they might find.

Willow burst through the door of the tiny hut. There sat Kiaya, calmly feeding the baby. They were safe!

Relieved, Willow hugged his wife, then told her what had happened. "We can't keep this to ourselves any longer, Kiaya. We must take the baby to the village council."

A town meeting was called. Willow nervously shoved his way through the excited, frightened crowd.

"One Death Dog we can kill!" shouted Burglekutt. "But there may be more. And Bavmorda's beasts won't give up the search till they find whatever it is they're looking for!"

"It's a sign!" someone shouted.

"There'll be another drought! Or a plague!" cried another.

"Who's to blame for this? Throw him into the pit!"

At that, Willow turned and headed for the back door.

"Willow Ufgood!" cried the High Aldwin. "Come forward."

The crowd parted to let Willow pass. "High Aldwin," he said. "My children found this Daikini baby in the river."

"That's what the beast wanted!"

cried Burglekutt. "The baby! It's not one of us—give it to the dogs!"

"But they'll kill her!" Willow protested.

The High Aldwin called for silence. Then he gently laid his hands upon the baby and closed his eyes. "A Daikini baby . . . of some strange destiny, I feel." He paused, as if listening to some distant voice. "Yes . . . I sense this child is . . . special."

Suddenly the High Aldwin dropped his arms and opened his eyes. The villagers waited silently for the magician's words. Finally he spoke: "The child must be taken beyond the boundaries of our village. Far across the great river, to the Daikini crossroads!"

Everyone gasped. Who would dare venture that far?

Burglekutt's eyes glowed with an idea. If Willow were sent on this dangerous mission, he might not come back. Then Burglekutt could take over Willow's land! So he spoke up. "It seems only fair that the man to take this baby to the crossroads be the man who found it. I nominate Willow Ufgood!"

"But I have my crops to put in!" cried Willow.

"I will consult the bones!" the High Aldwin said. The crowd watched breathlessly as the sorcerer scattered a handful of dry bones across the floor. He studied them silently for a moment. He scratched his head. Then he whispered to Willow, "The bones tell me nothing. But I must make a decision. Do you have any love for this child?"

Willow looked at the baby. "Yes," he said softly.

"The bones have spoken!" the High Aldwin announced to the crowd. "Willow—the security of this village depends on you!"

Burglekutt grinned smugly as the crowd cheered.

"But you will need help!" the High Aldwin added. "The outer world is a dangerous and corrupt place, and this baby is hunted by bloodthirsty beasts. Who has the courage to join Willow on his journey?"

Vohnkar the warrior stepped forward. "I'll go!"

Burglekutt turned white. "No! Not Vohnkar! He's our best warrior. We need him here to protect us!"

But no one else volunteered. Finally Willow's friend Meegosh stepped forward. "I'll go with Willow!"

"Excellent! Praise the bones!" cried Burglekutt, smiling.

The High Aldwin frowned at Burglekutt. Then an idea came to him, and he smiled. "Now all we need is someone to lead the way. And according to the bones, that leader is— Burglekutt!"

Back at Nockmaar Castle, Bavmorda raged at her daughter. "I didn't ask you to bring me a dead nursemaid! Sorsha, you useless—"

"The baby can't be far from where we found the midwife. I'll find her," answered Sorsha.

Suddenly a huge figure filled the doorway and stepped forward.

"General Kael!" Bavmorda greeted the cruel-faced warrior. "Help my daughter find this tiny, helpless baby that somehow continues to elude her."

She cast a scornful look at Sorsha, who grew pale.

"The baby of the prophecy?" asked Kael. "The one who would destroy you?"

"I need that baby alive," said Bavmorda. "I must perform the ritual that will send the child's spirit into oblivion. Find her!"

"I don't need his help, Mother!" cried Sorsha.

"You'll do as I say, *child*!" ordered Bavmorda.

Two bright red spots appeared on Sorsha's cheeks, but she controlled her anger. She nodded to Kael, and they left Bavmorda's chamber.

One of Bavmorda's Druids stepped out of the shadows. "One day, I fear, your daughter will betray you," he said.

"Then I will crush her," said Bavmorda, a cold, terrible light in her eyes.

At sunrise the next day in the Nelwyn village the small band gathered on a sacred hill: Willow, his friend Meegosh, Burglekutt, Vohnkar, and several of the village's best warriors.

Kiaya, a kerchief wrapped around her head, handed the baby to Willow. "Take care of her, and don't worry about us. We'll be fine. I know you are doing the right thing." Then she put a braid of hair into his hand. "This will bring you luck."

"You cut your hair!" Willow gasped. He hugged his wife close for a long moment. Then he kissed his children. It was hard to say goodbye, for he had never been away from his family before.

"Good, brave people," said the High Aldwin, "the outer world is no place for a Nelwyn. It is a land where weapons mean more than plowshares, and where giants fight among themselves, destroying the lives and land of many innocent creatures unlucky enough to stand in their way. I tell you to give this baby to the first Daikini you see. Then hurry home, where you belong."

"All right, men, move it out!" Burglekutt commanded.

But the High Aldwin pulled Willow aside. "When I held up my fingers yesterday, what did you first think to answer?"

"Oh, it was stupid. . . ." said Willow.

"Just tell me!"

"I first thought to pick my own finger."

The High Aldwin shook his head. "You lack faith in yourself, Willow. More than anyone in this village, you have the potential to be a great sorcerer. You must learn to listen to your own heart, to trust your own intuition." Then he gave Willow a handful of acorns. "Anything you hurl these at will turn to stone. Use them wisely."

"Ufgood!" shouted Burglekutt. "Hurry up, you lazy lout!"

"I'd love to throw one at Burglekutt. . . ." Willow muttered as he hurried after the others into the unknown.

It was not an easy journey, for they were stalked by strange animals and slept on the cold ground. Finally, nearing exhaustion, they came to their destination—a place in the wilderness where two huge roads crossed.

The Daikini crossroads was deserted. A few broken wagon wheels lay on the ground. Several prison cages, littered with bones, hung from ancient scaffolding for all who passed to see.

Vohnkar and his men built a fire. Meegosh unpacked supplies. Willow fed the baby and rocked it to sleep.

Soon the world beyond their small circle of firelight disappeared in the evening shadows. One by one the night sounds joined into a spooky chorus: the chirp of crickets, the hoot of owls, and the howling of distant wolves.

Then came a terrible groan.

"I hate this," said Willow grimly. Suddenly he felt a hand grab his collar and yank him into the air! Willow screamed as he was pulled up against the rough wooden bars of one of the prison cages. There was somebody inside!

"Get me some water, or you'll di-i-i-ie!" the prisoner shouted, his savage eyes and teeth inches from Willow's face.

"Anything you say," said Willow, gasping for breath.

As soon as he was dropped to the ground, Willow hurried to pick up the baby. Then Vohnkar and his men approached, their weapons drawn.

"Hey, you weaselly little cheats! Get me some water!" the prisoner roared, thrashing wildly against his cage.

"We're in luck!" exclaimed Burglekutt. "He's a Daikini!"

Willow was horrified. "We can't give the baby to him!"

"We have to give the baby to somebody. . . ." said Vohnkar.

The prisoner grinned. Maybe *this*

was his ticket to freedom! "I'm somebody! Let me out and I'll take care
of her." He made funny faces, and
she giggled. "See? She likes me."

"I trust him completely," said Burglekutt. "Let's go."

But Willow refused to give up the
child. The prisoner was a criminal, a
madman. Who knew what he'd do to
the baby!

"Listen, runt," Burglekutt said to
Willow, "our orders were to give the
baby to the first Daikini we saw. I'm

in charge here, and I say we go—
now!"

The others agreed. Only Meegosh
took Willow's side and chose to re-
main with him.

"Fools!" laughed Burglekutt, and
he led the others away.

"Wait!" cried the prisoner. "Come
back! Let me out of here!"

"What do we do now?" Meegosh
asked Willow as the night wind howled
spookily through the trees.

"Wait for somebody else to come

along, I guess," said Willow. He sat as far from the prisoner as he could and eyed him suspiciously, until he fell asleep with the baby in his arms.

The next morning Willow and Meegosh were awakened by the sound of hoofbeats. A military messenger galloped by.

"What's going on?" said Willow.

"Smells like a battle," said the prisoner.

"And I suppose you're an expert," said Willow.

"Didn't I introduce myself?" asked the prisoner. "Madmartigan. The greatest swordsman that ever lived."

"Gee, Willow, maybe he could help us," said Meegosh.

"These are bad times, my friend," Madmartigan said to Meegosh. "Good men like me locked in cages, criminals running free. It doesn't pay to be honest in Queen Bavmorda's world. . . . You a woodcutter?"

"Miner. And my friend's a farmer."

"I knew it!" said Madmartigan. "Victims of a rotten corrupt world, just like me. We need to stick together!"

"Don't listen to him," Willow said to Meegosh. "Who knows *what* he's done to get himself locked up in there!"

Suddenly they heard the sound of a hundred horses. And then a huge army of Daikinis rode into view.

Willow ran up to the officer in charge. "Sir! sir! We found one of your babies in our village. Will you take her?"

The huge soldier glared down from his horse. "We're going into battle, little one. Find a woman to take care of it!"

Madmartigan rocked against his cage. "They thought *you* were a woman, Airk Thaughbaer!"

"Well, I'll be," said the soldier.

"Madmartigan! I knew you'd end up in a crow's cage. What did you do this time?"

"Nothing you wouldn't have done in my place," said Madmartigan. "What are you doing this far north?"

"Bavmorda's army is on a rampage," explained Airk. He was the leader of the rebel army, sworn to defeat Queen Bavmorda. "They're searching for someone and destroying everything in their path. We're going to try to stop them at River Troon."

"Let me out—I'll win this war for you!" Madmartigan cried.

Airk laughed. "After that stunt at Land's End you're lucky I don't kill you! You told me you serve no one. Remember? So stay in your coffin and rot!" And he galloped off to rejoin his soldiers.

Willow and Meegosh continued to wait for someone who would take the baby. Normally the Daikini crossroads was a busy place. But no one came by. Today the distant sounds of battle sent even the animals into their hiding places.

"Look, nobody's going to take care of your baby," said Madmartigan from his cage. "You know why? There's a war on. Nobody cares about one little baby when whole villages are in trouble. You want to go home? Just let me out, and I'll take care of the baby—maybe even find its mother. I swear on my honor as a soldier that I'll look after it like it was my own!"

"I believe he would," said Meegosh. "And he *is* a Daikini."

Willow still wasn't sure. But he did have his fields to plow and his own family to take care of. And Madmartigan didn't look half as bad in the light of day as he had by firelight. The baby seemed to like him all right. . . .

Finally Willow agreed.

"But you've got to promise to feed her, and change her often," he said as Meegosh hacked open the cage door.

"No problem!" said Madmartigan cheerily. And he marched off singing

battle songs with the baby bouncing happily in the pack on his back.

Willow and Meegosh hurried along the path toward their village. What heroes they would be when they got home!

"We did the right thing, didn't we?" asked Willow.

"Absolutely. Nothing to worry about," Meegosh assured him.

Then out of the blue a giant eagle swooped by—clutching a crying baby in its claws.

"Hey! That's our baby!" cried Willow.

Sitting atop the bird was a tiny, laughing brownie. Willow knew all about brownies. Nelwyn children grew up hearing tales of their mischievous pranks and magic.

Frantically Willow and Meegosh chased after the bird. They raced through the thickening forest until— they tumbled into the pit of a brownie's trap. And everything went black.

✳   ✳   ✳

Willow woke as a tiny pail of water splashed his face. His hands and feet were tied, and he and Meegosh were surrounded by dozens of brownies with painted faces and spiky hair. Around them little bonfires burned against the night.

The brownie who had ridden the eagle stepped forward. He was no taller than a daisy. "I am Franjean, King of the World!"

That sent all the other brownies into fits of giggles.

"Where's the baby?" cried Willow.

Franjean whacked Willow on the nose. "Quiet, fool! I'm not afraid of you Nelwyns. You think you're so big!"

Just then, overhead, the trees swayed with a wind-borne voice. "Franjean, bring the Nelwyn to me. . . ."

"Uh-oh, that's Cherlindrea, queen of the fairies," said a brownie named Rool. He wagged a finger at Willow. "You're in big trouble now!"

With fairies dancing around their

heads like fireflies, the brownies dragged Willow deep into the woods.

"Release the Nelwyn!" ordered the voice.

At once the brownies cut Willow's ropes. As he stood a strange light began to glow among the trees, brighter and brighter, until he could see the baby asleep in a tiny cradle. Then, as light flooded the forest, a beautiful, luminous being appeared—Cherlindrea.

"Welcome to my kingdom, Willow Ufgood," she said.

"How do you know my name?" Willow asked, astonished.

"Elora Danan told me," Cherlin-drea said, looking toward the cradle. "Elora, Willow's here. . . ."

"But she's just a baby!" said Willow. "She can't talk."

Cherlindrea smiled. "Elora is not an ordinary baby. I can hear what is in her thoughts . . . and in her heart."

"So she *is* special!" said Willow, smiling at the baby with reverent affection. "I knew she was. And now she has a fairy queen to protect her. I guess I can go on home."

"No, Willow," said Cherlindrea. "Your journey has just begun. Elora Danan has chosen you to be her guardian."

Willow caught Elora as she floated

Cherlindrea's light intensified, and she swirled around Willow like a luminous wind. "Elora Danan must survive! Only she can bring about the downfall of Queen Bavmorda!"

Then there was silence—and darkness.

Willow stood blinking in the pale light of the moon as Cherlindrea's voice echoed into the night: "All creatures of good heart need your help, Willow. Soon Bavmorda will control your village, the lives of your children . . . everyone. I cannot make you go. The choice is yours. . . ."

At dawn Willow made his choice. He had thought long and hard throughout the night, and he knew in his heart that he must face the challenge of this journey. For Elora. And for everyone he loved. But he would not let his good friend risk his life too. Gently he woke Meegosh. "Go home," Willow told him. "Tell my family I'll be all right . . . and that I love them very much."

Once again Willow set off into the woods. Cherlindrea sent two brownies, Rool and Franjean, to help him find the sorceress Fin Raziel.

After days of hiking through the rain, they came to a roadside tavern. They went inside to get Elora some milk.

The dark, smoky great room upstairs was packed with people—traveling merchants, mothers with babies, cutthroats, thieves—most of them twice as big as Willow. Crowded and shoved into a corner, he leaned against

from the cradle. Then Cherlindrea gave Willow what looked like an old twig.

"Take my magic wand to the sorceress Fin Raziel. Bavmorda exiled her to a lonely island in the middle of a lake a few days' journey over the hills. Only Fin Raziel can help you guard Elora against the dangers to come."

"Oh, no, not me!" said Willow. "Why can't you go? You've got magical powers."

"I wish I could," Cherlindrea said sadly. "But my powers do not extend beyond this forest."

Willow pleaded with the baby, "You don't want me, Elora. You need a powerful warrior or a real magician who can protect you. I'm nobody. I'm short—even for a Nelwyn!"

the wall—and tumbled through a rotting plank into the next room.

Embarrassed, Willow peeked over an unmade bed. The brownies, clinging to his collar, peeked out from behind his ears. They saw two women dressing in a hurry. One was quite pretty. The other was pretty . . . ugly.

"Hurry, he's coming!" said the pretty one.

The ugly one was frantically piling on gobs of makeup. "How do I look?" she asked—in a deep, *masculine* voice.

Willow jumped up. "Like a dirty rotten scoundrel!"

The ugly one turned. Beneath the kerchief, beneath all the makeup, that rascally face was unmistakable—Madmartigan!

"Where'd you come from?" Madmartigan exclaimed.

"I knew I shouldn't have trusted you—" Willow began.

"Wait!" said Madmartigan. "I can explain—"

But their reunion was cut short as the bedroom door slammed open. In stormed a huge man.

"This is Llug," the real woman said. "My husband."

"How do you do?" said Madmartigan in a high, giggly voice.

The jealous-eyed Llug stopped, a confused look on his face. He had expected to catch his wife with another man. Before he could figure things out, Madmartigan grabbed Elora from Willow's arms and headed for the door. "Dear me, these

Nelwyns make terrible nursemaids," he said, holding the protesting Willow at arm's length. "Oh well, time to go! Ta-ta!" And he sashayed out the door.

Three seconds later he backed into the room—at sword point. In the doorway stood Sorsha and three Nockmaar soldiers. Upstairs, the tavern was a madhouse, as brutal soldiers grabbed babies from their screaming mothers, searching for the child with the special birthmark.

"Is that your baby?" Sorsha demanded as she reached for Elora. But Madmartigan shoved her aside, knocking her helmet askew. Irritated, Sorsha pulled off her helmet, and her wild red hair tumbled down her shoulders.

For a moment Madmartigan forgot his disguise. "By glory, you're beautiful. . . ." he said in his natural deep voice.

"And you're awfully strong," said Sorsha. She squinted at him, then

yanked off his kerchief. "You're no woman!"

"Not a woman?!" growled Llug.

"Gentlemen," said the fast-talking Madmartigan, "meet Llug!" He ducked as Llug's fist met a soldier's face!

Then, gathering his skirts, Madmartigan leaped through the window with Elora Danan still in his arms.

"Madmartiga-a-a-a-n!" yelled Willow, tumbling after him with the brownies clinging to his sleeves. They just barely landed in a horse cart

below as Madmartigan giddyapped the horse, and they all bolted toward the woods.

The rickety wagon careened forward at a dizzying speed. The brownies clung to each other, trying not to bounce off, and Willow struggled to sit up. He found a small box filled with straw and placed Elora safely inside it.

"Stop this wagon, Madmartigan!" yelled Willow. "You're going to get us killed!" He leaned over the driver's seat and grabbed for the reins.

"What are you doing? Are you crazy?" hollered Madmartigan. The huge Daikini warrior tightened his grip on the reins as the wagon hit a terrific bump. Willow tumbled backward into the cart.

They had a good head start. Then all of a sudden Madmartigan pulled the horse to a standstill. "*Now* we stop, Nelwyn. Everybody out!" he hissed, and whacked the horse's rump, sending the wagon rattling down the road.

As the dust swirled around them, Madmartigan smiled with satisfaction. "You can go ahead and thank me now."

"Thank you?" sputtered Willow. "I should throttle you, you reckless hooligan! I knew I should never have trusted you! You swore on your honor you'd take care of the baby."

"I just saved that baby's life!" Madmartigan shouted.

The brownies stood aside as Willow and Madmartigan glared furiously at each other. Then the sound of approaching hoofbeats broke their deadlock. They all scrambled into a nearby ditch, where they lay hidden as Sorsha and her troops thundered past.

As soon as the coast was clear, Willow spoke up. "First you lose the baby. Then you drive like a maniac—with an *infant* in the wagon! You are no man of honor," he said to Madmartigan.

"I was once the greatest knight in the kingdom of Galladoorn," snarled Madmartigan. He picked up a long stick and swished it through the air like an imaginary sword. But he was so angry that he lost his hold. The stick flew through the air.

Willow stood with his arms folded across his chest. "You're reckless," he said.

"And dangerous," added Rool.

"I say we execute him!" voted Franjean.

Madmartigan had had quite enough. "Who needs this? I'm leaving to find some people my own size!" He strode away, turning only to blow a kiss at Elora Danan, who giggled happily.

Willow looked at the brownies. Rool hiccuped so hard he lost his balance and fell over. Franjean almost fell trying to help Rool up. Elora Danan began to cry. Willow straightened his shoulders and took off after Madmartigan, clutching the baby in his arms.

"Madmartigan, wait!" he called.

"Go home, Willow," said Madmartigan. "I thought you didn't trust me."

"I don't," said Willow. "But we need your help. I . . . I apologize for losing my temper. You *did* save our lives back there. You're a great warrior and a swordsman, and you're ten times bigger than me. Please, Madmartigan."

Madmartigan squinted down at Elora. Then he stroked her fuzzy baby hair. "Which way are you headed?" he finally asked Willow.

The two brownies popped up, one on either side of Madmartigan.

"This way," said Rool, pointing toward the woods.

"Beyond those hills, to the lake!" said Franjean.

Madmartigan sighed. "All right, all right. That's the way I'm going too. . . . But only as far as the lake!"

It was not the most pleasant journey. Madmartigan and the brownies kept picking at each other. Willow and Madmartigan argued like rival grandfathers about everything from diapering techniques to whether it was good or bad to let Elora teethe on blackroot.

Eventually, though, they arrived safely at the lake. In the distance a small island shimmered in the mist over the water.

"That's where we'll find Fin Raziel," said Rool.

"Looks like you don't need me anymore," said Madmartigan. "I'm off to join the fighting."

"Madmartigan!" Willow called after him.

"What?" answered the Daikini warrior.

"Thanks."

With a jaunty wave and a grin Madmartigan was gone.

Willow found a boat and pushed it toward the lake. But he was afraid to take Elora Danan with him. Reluctantly he left her with the brownies on the shore. Then he rowed toward the misty island alone.

When, not long after, his boat

bumped ashore near a broken skeleton, a tiny, possumlike animal was watching him from a tree. "Who are you?" it chattered. "What are you doing here?"

"I am Willow Ufgood. I'm here to find the great sorceress Fin Raziel," Willow answered.

The possum proudly raised its nose in the air. "*I* am Fin Raziel." Then she added sadly, "Bavmorda cast a spell on me."

Willow, trying hard to hide his dismay, showed her Cherlindrea's wand and told her of Elora Danan.

As he spoke, a flock of birds screeched through the sky. The wind began to howl. The sky darkened with thunderclouds.

"Hide the wand!" cried Raziel. "Bavmorda knows of your presence here! We must leave this island immediately!"

Willow quickly carried the little possum to the boat, then pushed off into the stormy waves. Though the storm died down as they reached the opposite shore, Willow's troubles were far from over.

As soon as he and Raziel landed on the bank, they were surrounded by Nockmaar soldiers on horseback. One held the crying baby, stolen from the brownies, who cowered nearby. And there on another horse was Madmartigan. Willow could not believe it. Had Madmartigan betrayed him again?

"Sorry about this," Madmartigan said with a weak smile.

"Keep your mouth shut!" yelled a soldier, who brutally knocked Madmartigan from his horse. As Madmartigan lay facedown in the dirt Willow saw that his hands were bound, his shirt torn, his back bloody with whip marks. He was a prisoner again.

"See?" spat the soldier. "You couldn't stop us. We found them anyway!"

One soldier caught Raziel by the tail. Another grabbed Willow by the scruff of the neck just as Sorsha galloped up. She grabbed the baby and pulled open the blanket so she could see Elora's tiny arm.

"There's the mark—this is the baby we're looking for," she said. "We must take it back to Nockmaar Castle."

Sorsha's eyes fell upon Madmartigan. "Lose your dress?" she asked sarcastically.

Madmartigan struggled to his feet. "You ever thought of disguising *yourself* as a woman?" he answered.

Swift as lightning, Sorsha landed a punch on Madmartigan's jaw that sent him sprawling again. Then, with a toss of her fiery curls, she leaped onto her mount. Her guards gathered the prisoners and followed as she spurred her horse toward the snow-topped mountains—and the Nockmaar camp.

Rool and Franjean looked after

Sorsha and her soldiers in dismay.

"We can't keep up with them," said Rool. "Even if we could, they'd catch us, torture us, and finally devour us."

"Are you suggesting we go home?" asked Franjean.

"Of course not!" said Rool. "This is much more fun!"

And they chased after the soldiers.

That night, in the darkness of a prison cage in the Nockmaar mountain camp, Raziel whispered to Willow, "You must use the wand to restore me to my human form so we can save Elora."

"All right. What do I do first?"

Raziel began to teach Willow some instant magic. "Repeat after me," she coached. "But don't let anything break your concentration."

Willow raised the wand. Shyly he began to chant the unfamiliar words: "Hither greenan . . . uh . . . bairn claideb lunanockt . . ."

Suddenly the brownies squeezed through the bars of the cage. "Hello, everybody—we're here!" cried Franjean.

"You're saved!" shouted Rool heroically.

"*Quiet!*" Madmartigan and Raziel hissed at once.

Willow cleared his throat. This wasn't going to be so easy. He began to chant again: "Avaggdu . . . suporium . . . um . . . luatha . . ."

"Concentrate, Willow!" Raziel coached—in a strangely squawking voice. Her body twisted. Slowly her brown fur grew into . . . black feathers! Raziel had turned into a bird!

Willow collapsed and dropped the smoking wand.

"Whoops, the Nelwyn made a mess out of that one!" giggled Rool.

Willow was downcast. "Now we'll never get out."

"Sure we will," said Rool. "We can pick the lock!" He and Franjean scurried up the bars and poked at the lock with their tiny spears.

"Here, let me try," said Madmartigan.

"Stand back, big guy!" cried Franjean. He whacked Madmartigan in the face with his shoulder pouch, and a strange dust billowed out into the air. Madmartigan sneezed as the dust filled his eyes and nose.

"What's *that*?" whispered Rool.

"It's Dust of Broken Heart," Fran-jean whispered back. "I kind of borrowed it from the fairies. It's supposed to make him fall in love with the next woman he sees."

But by then the door had swung open, and Willow was dragging the dizzy-looking Madmartigan out into the dark night. "Aren't the stars bee-*yoo*-tiful tonight?" Madmartigan said dreamily, gazing into the sky.

"Come on, Madmartigan, snap out of it!" cried Willow. "We've got to find Elora!"

They reached Sorsha's tent and peeked in. There was Elora, not far from where Sorsha lay sleeping.

"Better let an expert do this," insisted Madmartigan, and he slipped in under the canvas. Inside, he crawled on hands and knees past Sorsha. In a nightgown instead of armor, with her copper-colored tresses coiling across

her pillow, she looked more like a goddess than a soldier. Madmartigan stifled a sneeze and rubbed at his eyes. A strange look crossed his face.

Rool giggled. "Dust of Broken Heart strikes again!"

"Sorsha!" Madmartigan cried suddenly. "I love you!"

Instantly Sorsha was awake, her dagger at Madmartigan's throat. "Get away from me!" she cried.

"You are my moon, my sun, my starlit sky—" He kissed the hand that held the knife. "My heart is pounding!"

"I can fix that!" said Sorsha. "I'll put a knife through it!" But then she looked into his eyes. And the knife dropped from her hand. Madmartigan was about to kiss her—

"What's going on here?!" In the doorway stood General Kael, second only to Sorsha in Bavmorda's army. In one hand he gripped a scowling Willow. In the other he clutched Elora.

"Liar!" Sorsha shouted at Madmartigan. Then everyone lunged at once—and the tent collapsed around them.

The entire camp awoke in confusion as Madmartigan and Willow, holding Elora, crawled out. Half-dressed soldiers ran helter-skelter through the predawn darkness.

In the confusion a shield skidded across the snow.

"Willow! Jump on!" cried Madmartigan. As archers drew their bows Madmartigan and Willow dived onto the shield and flew down the icy mountainside. They shrieked in terror. The brownies held on for dear life. Raziel flapped after them, squawking a blue streak. And Elora Danan laughed with delight as they left the soldiers far behind.

At the foot of the mountain they plowed into a snowdrift near a small village. Madmartigan blinked and looked around. The tumble seemed to have knocked some sense into his

head—or some fairy dust out—because he was very angry when Willow and the brownies began to tease him about his romantic outburst. "You're all crazy!" he said. "I hate that woman . . . don't I?"

In the village they once again met Airk Thaughbaer, the rebel leader they had seen at the Daikini crossroads. His tattered band of soldiers was hiding out, to rest from a recent battle with a legion of Bavmorda's soldiers.

"I knew you'd figure a way out of that cage!" said Airk.

"You left me to die!" spat Madmartigan, his fist raised.

"Hey, now, save your energy for the real enemy," said Airk. Then his voice softened. "Besides, I probably saved your life. Bavmorda's soldiers slaughtered us that day. I lost many brave men. . . ."

In Willow's arms the baby began to babble. "Still carrying around that baby, I see. Who is it, anyway?"

"She's a queen," explained Willow.

"Or at least she will be when she grows up. Bavmorda wants to kill her. We're trying to get to a place where Bavmorda can't find the baby, where she'll be safe and well cared for."

Airk looked stunned. "*No one* can hide from Bavmorda's army!"

"We've managed it so far," said Madmartigan. "Don't forget that I'm a skilled warrior."

Airk looked at Madmartigan as if he were crazy. "I've lost half my men fighting Bavmorda. Now you and this little fool are going to take her on? You've always said you serve no one, Madmartigan. Since when did you become a crusader?"

"Well, maybe now I serve the Nelwyn—and his infant queen," said Madmartigan. It was difficult to tell who was most surprised by his declaration: Willow, Airk—or Madmartigan himself. "Want to join us?" he asked Airk.

"You'll never make it," Airk said quietly.

"Then once again we say goodbye."

The sun climbed high in the sky as Madmartigan and Willow rode borrowed horses beyond the snows, with Raziel flying ahead to lead the way. Soon they came to a lush valley of flowers. In the distance stood a beautiful castle.

"It's the castle of Tir Asleen!" cried Raziel. "Elora will be safe here. These are a good and noble people."

"Are you sure?" asked Willow nervously. "It looks awfully quiet."

Indeed, as the small party approached they heard no sound. For throughout the castle, the people of Tir Asleen stood trapped inside crystal statues.

"Bavmorda has cursed the castle!" squawked Raziel, flying overhead. "Quickly, Willow, try again to transform me. Then I shall see if I can do something to break this spell."

Again Willow raised the magic wand. No sooner had he begun to chant than a noise made him turn. Through the castle's open gates he saw Kael and his army trampling through the valley of flowers, their weapons drawn.

"Willow!" Raziel screamed. "Concentrate!"

But it was too late. Raziel had turned into a goat!

Meanwhile Madmartigan had found the castle's arsenal of weapons and was preparing the castle for battle. He donned a suit of golden armor,

closed and barred the gates, and set up scores of hair-trigger booby traps throughout the courtyard. Then he and Willow hauled a huge catapult into position.

All too soon came a thundering noise: Nockmaar soldiers battering down the gates! As Madmartigan prepared to face them Willow climbed onto one of the castle's towers to hide the baby.

Suddenly a hairy troll jumped in front of him, smacking its hungry lips. The baby screamed. Willow pulled a magic acorn from his pocket, threw it—and missed!

"Willow! Use the wand!" Raziel cried from below.

And he did—he used it to crack the troll on the head! "Avaggdu strockt!"

he shouted. The troll disintegrated into a blob of jiggling jelly. With a disgusted shudder, Willow kicked it into the moat. "I hate this," he said.

Below, the Nockmaar soldiers splintered the huge gates and swarmed inside. Madmartigan fought with the skill of a thousand generals, but slowly his enemies backed him toward the moat. He brandished his sword, ready to die fighting.

Suddenly the soldiers backed off. Madmartigan grinned. "Scared of ol' Mad, eh?" Then a blood curdling sound behind him made him turn.

The murky waters of the moat boiled around a giant, two-headed Eborsisk belching fire from its jaws!

* * *

As Madmartigan and the Nock-maar soldiers fought the beast, Sorsha wandered through the castle. Strangely, she did not feel like joining in the battle. For weeks she had thought of nothing but her relentless search for the infant Elora.

Now she remembered the baby's tiny softness when it lay beside her in her tent at the Nockmaar camp. The child must be nearby, yet Sorsha made no move to find her.

Sorsha touched the icy cold of the crystal statues. These people had once lived and breathed, worked and laughed . . . and now Bavmorda had imprisoned them with a horrifying enchantment. What had they done to deserve this?

Across the courtyard, she knew, the cruel General Kael was ordering his soldiers to their deaths in the service of Bavmorda's evil. Sorsha winced as she thought of her mother's terrifying, unforgiving temper. Then she thought of Madmartigan, standing alone against Bavmorda's soldiers to protect a Nelwyn and a helpless infant. . . .

At the moat she saw him, in golden armor, drop onto the neck of the Eborsisk and drive his sword through one of the monster's skulls. As Madmartigan tumbled to safe ground the beast tried to blow fire through its pinned jaws—and exploded into fireworks that sizzled as they rained into the waters of the moat.

Madmartigan lay on the ground, dazed. Then his eyes focused on a pair of grimy boots. He looked up into the impassive face of Sorsha, who stood with her sword drawn, its steely tip inches from Madmartigan's throat. He prepared to meet his death.

For a moment they stared into each other's eyes. Then Sorsha smiled, pulled him to his feet—and into her arms.

✻　✻　✻

General Kael saw Sorsha's change of heart—and cursed her. But he, at least, had gotten what he'd come for. Climbing onto his horse, he held Elora Danan high above his head and shouted against the wind: "Troops! To Nockmaar Castle!"

As their hoofbeats faded, others grew louder. On the horizon Airk Thaughbaer and hundreds of rebel horsemen charged toward Tir Asleen. And poking out of Airk's saddlebags were Rool and Franjean, waving their tiny spears with glee!

"Out for a ride in the country, Airk?" Madmartigan called.

"Thought you might get lonely way out here," shouted Airk, laughing. But when he spotted Bavmorda's daughter, he drew his sword.

Madmartigan stepped between them. "Sorsha rides with me."

Then Willow staggered from the castle, tears streaking his face. "They got Elora! I tried to protect her. . . . I tried to fight, but there were too many of them. . . ."

"Don't worry—we'll save her," Madmartigan said as he scooped his little friend up into the saddle. Then, at a signal from Airk, the rebel soldiers spurred their horses toward Nockmaar Castle, with Raziel the goat clip-clopping along behind them.

* * *

It was dark when the rebel forces set up camp below Nockmaar Castle. Above them, in a dark tower, they heard Elora Danan cry. Bavmorda appeared at the parapet, silhouetted in eerie torchlight, and her laughter echoed down the mountainside.

Suddenly Raziel, still a goat, butted Willow into a tent. "Quick!" she told him. "The shelter chant! Protect yourself!"

Without question, Willow obeyed. "Helgafel swaathben helgafel . . ."

Outside, Madmartigan shouted, "Give us Elora Danan!"

"You dare to challenge me?" Bavmorda cried. "You're not soldiers—you're pigs! Nocklith! Vohkbar! Toa thonna mondarr!"

Her spell turned the rebels into *real* pigs!

Inside his tent Willow was still chanting. "You can stop now," said Raziel. "It's safe. You did well."

Willow opened his eyes. Bavmorda's spell had not touched him or Raziel. He had worked real magic! But when he saw the army of pigs outside, his spirits fell. "I've come all this way, and still Elora Danan's going to die."

"We *can* defeat Bavmorda," said Raziel. "But it's up to you, Willow. If you transform me, I can destroy her."

Willow's hand shook, and he fumbled with the wand. "It's just no use! I can't do it! I'm not a sorcerer!"

"But you can be—and you must!" said Raziel. "Reach deep into your heart, Willow. Speak—and be one with the words."

Willow gazed up at Queen Bavmorda's castle. Somewhere inside was the baby, his precious Elora. She had chosen *him* to be her champion, Cherlindrea had said. Now he had the chance to save her and save the world from a future darkened by the queen's evil. . . .

Willow firmly gripped the wand. He closed his eyes and emptied his mind of everything but the magic. Then he began to chant in a voice that was clear and strong, "Locktwarr danalora luatha danu, tuatha tuatha, chnox danu . . ."

And suddenly Raziel was changing, first into a grotesque, half-formed creature, then into a deer, and slowly into a human. Willow fought to control the magic, to let it live through

him. Finally, Raziel was herself again, a silver-haired sorceress.

"Willow, you did it," she said, embracing him as he blinked back tears of joy.

Then, with the quick mastery born of years of magic, Raziel changed the pigs back into soldiers.

Everyone argued about what to do next.

Willow spoke up. "Back in my village we catch a lot of gophers. They ruin our fields—"

"Willow, this is war, not agriculture," said Madmartigan.

"I know. But this may help us get into the castle."

They gathered together to hear Willow's idea.

"Too much work to finish by morning!" said Airk.

"General Kael will never fall for it," said Sorsha.

Even Madmartigan was skeptical.

But Raziel was willing to try. "If Elora dies, all hope for the future dies with her. I'm going to fight!"

"Me too!" said Willow.

Madmartigan called for silence. "We must decide: Who's going to leave and who's going to stay? . . ."

The next morning the sun rose on a deserted battleground. Only Raziel and Willow stood before the castle.

"We are powerful sorcerers!" Willow called up to the tower. "Give us the baby or we will destroy you."

The drawbridge lowered. Only a handful of snickering horsemen rode out to deal with the runt and the old lady.

Willow waited till they were close. Then he turned and pounded a war drum, which echoed across the land-scape.

Madmartigan leaped out of the ground on horseback! Then Sorsha appeared. And Airk! Then the entire rebel army clambered to life from endless pits and trenches and stormed past the stunned soldiers and into the castle.

Inside, Madmartigan and Airk plunged into the fight like brothers while Sorsha led Willow and Raziel up the gloomy winding stairs of Bavmorda's tower. At the top Raziel waved the wand, and the door creaked open.

Bavmorda peered over her shoulder at them. Her face crinkled into a crazed smile. "Good. I'm glad you've come. You can witness my greatest triumph!" She stepped aside and pointed a tal-oned finger. Before her Elora Danan lay on a raised stone altar in a death-like trance. The ritual had already begun!

"No!" Sorsha cried. "I won't let you destroy this child."

"Traitor! I warned you not to op-pose me!" Bavmorda snarled. She spat out a curse that hurled Sorsha at a spike-covered wall. But another force caught the unconscious girl and gently lowered her to the floor.

"You've gained strength, Raziel," Bavmorda hissed, magically hurling a battle-ax at her rival.

"I have Cherlindrea's wand," Ra-ziel countered as she froze the ax in midair. "You cannot defeat our com-bined power. Elora Danan will be queen!"

The two powerful sorceresses faced each other. The air crackled as their potent energies—good and evil—clashed in an unearthly fight. Bavmorda concentrated on the huge

stone gargoyles on the walls of her chamber, and they sprang into ferocious life. Raziel pointed her wand, and the gargoyles exploded into a shower of dust. Fireballs flew. The room spun with flying objects and cascading sparks.

Unnoticed amid the chaos, Willow inched toward the altar.

Suddenly a stone pillar toppled, pinning Raziel. The wand rolled across the floor and out of her reach, halving her power. Cackling, Bavmorda choked the weakened Raziel till she fell limp, unconscious. But before Bavmorda could destroy her, she heard a sound. She turned. Willow had the baby!

Bavmorda flicked her fingers and the door slammed shut. She towered over Willow. "And who, pray tell, are you?"

"I am Willow Ufgood, a great sorcerer," Willow said, with all the conviction he could muster. "Greater than Raziel—" He gulped. "Greater than you!"

Bavmorda threw back her head and laughed. Willow dug into his pocket. He still had some magic acorns left. He found one—and threw it.

Bavmorda caught it in her fist. Trembling, Willow held his breath. Instantly her hand turned to stone. Then her wrist, her arm, her shoulder . . .

Willow almost shouted with triumph!

Then his smile melted. Bavmorda's body shook as she fought the magic. Her evil will was strong. Slowly her stone shoulder turned back

into flesh. Then her arm, her wrist, her hand. . . . She crushed the acorn and let the dust trickle through her fingers.

"Is that the extent of your magic?" she asked dryly. "Now—watch *me*! I shall draw upon the energy of the universe to send that child into eternal darkness!"

"No!" shouted Willow. "You cannot have her. I'll use my magic, and I'll send her . . ." He groped for words.

"You're no sorcerer!" Bavmorda smirked.

Willow's face lit up with an idea. "I shall use my magic to send her to a place where evil cannot touch her!"

"What?!" cried Bavmorda. "There *is* no such place!"

Willow waved his arms dramatically and began to chant: "Helgafel swath ben helgafel, bairn off danu famoww . . ."

"What a silly fool!" muttered Bavmorda. She turned away for an instant to command the magic wand into her hand. When she turned back, Willow whirled his cape around himself, as if he were doing a magic trick at the Nelwyn spring festival.

And the baby was gone!

"Impossible!" gasped Bavmorda, her eyes wide with fury. In a rage she backed into the altar, spilling a bowl of luminous fluid to the floor, where it pooled around her boots. As the sky pulsed bright with the crackle of a storm, Bavmorda flew into a rage and shook the wand at the sky. Suddenly lightning zigzagged through the tower, seeking the wand as if it were a lightning rod.

And Bavmorda burst into flames!

Soon her screams faded, and a silence filled the tower. On the floor a light breeze teased at the pillar of ash, erasing forever all traces of the evil queen.

With a shout Madmartigan rammed open the door. He scooped the limp Sorsha into his arms and revived her with a kiss.

Raziel awoke in a panic. "Willow! Where is Elora Danan?!"

Willow just smiled and drew open his cloak. "This cloak is special," he explained. "Kiaya made it for me. It has a secret pocket. See here?" Gently he pulled out the baby. "You're safe now, Elora," he said, hugging her to his chest. "Queen Bavmorda is gone forever. I fooled her with my old disappearing-pig trick."

Elora's eyes fluttered open. She laughed. And sunlight flooded into the tower.

The next day the castle of Tir Asleen was alive once more with happy activity as the people celebrated the end of their enchantment. Then they gathered at the gates to bid Willow farewell. Sorsha held Elora Danan lovingly in her arms, with Madmartigan by her side. Willow knew that Elora would be well cared for.

Raziel presented Willow with an ancient book of sorcery. "You are well on your way to becoming a great sorcerer," she told him.

Willow kissed Elora Danan goodbye. Then suddenly he was flying— as Madmartigan lifted him into the saddle of a fine white pony.

"So long, little guy!" Madmartigan said with affection as he shook the Nelwyn's small hand.

Willow cantered off through the valley of flowers toward home.

* * *

As Willow approached the Nelwyn village he saw a celebration. The villagers lined the streets as musicians played a welcoming march. They were welcoming Willow like a hero!

Kiaya fought her way through the crowds. As soon as Willow caught sight of her, he leaped from his pony. They ran toward each other and embraced. Then Mims and Ranon jumped up to hug their father.

The High Aldwin came forward, beaming with pride. Willow smiled back. He reached into his saddlebag and took out an apple. Then Willow tossed the apple into the air. As the villagers watched in amazement it changed into a bird, which flew higher and higher above them.

Willow was home at last.